Dear Parent:

Your child's love of reading starts here!

Every child learns to read in a different way and at his or her own speed. Some go back and forth between reading levels and read favorite books again and again. Others read through each level in order. You can help your young reader improve and become more confident by encouraging his or her own interests and abilities. From books your child reads with you to the first books he or she reads alone, there are I Can Read Books for every stage of reading:

SHARED READING
Basic language, word repetition, and whimsical illustrations, ideal for sharing with your emergent reader

BEGINNING READING
Short sentences, familiar words, and simple concepts for children eager to read on their own

READING WITH HELP
Engaging stories, longer sentences, and language play for developing readers

READING ALONE
Complex plots, challenging vocabulary, and high-interest topics for the independent reader

I Can Read Books have introduced children to the joy of reading since 1957. Featuring award-winning authors and illustrators and a fabulous cast of beloved characters, I Can Read Books set the standard for beginning readers.

A lifetime of discovery begins with the magical words "I Can Read!"

Visit www.icanread.com for information
on enriching your child's reading experience.

I Can Read® and I Can Read Book® are trademarks of HarperCollins Publishers.

The Berenstain Bears Meet the Easter Bunny
Copyright © 2022 by Berenstain Publishing, Inc.
All rights reserved. Printed in the United States of America.
No part of this book may be used or reproduced in any manner whatsoever without written permission except
in the case of brief quotations embodied in critical articles and reviews. For information address HarperCollins
Children's Books, a division of HarperCollins Publishers, 195 Broadway, New York, NY 10007.
www.icanread.com

Library of Congress Control Number: 2021939651
ISBN 978-0-06-302447-2 (trade bdg.) — ISBN 978-0-06-302446-5 (pbk.)

21 22 23 24 25 LSCC 10 9 8 7 6 5 4 3 2 1 ❖ First Edition

I Can Read!

The Berenstain Bears®
Meet the
Easter Bunny

Mike Berenstain

Based on the characters created by
Stan and Jan Berenstain

HARPER
An Imprint of HarperCollinsPublishers

Easter is here!

The Bear family loves Easter.

They love the Easter Bunny.

The bears love Easter eggs!

They love Easter goodies!

The bears look for Easter eggs.

But they are not there!

8

The Easter Bunny did not come!

Where is the Easter Bunny?!

"Never mind!" says Papa.

"I will be the Easter Bunny!"

Papa puts on bunny ears.

He puts on bunny whiskers.

Papa gets a basket of eggs.

He hops around like a bunny.

"Happy Easter!" he calls.

But Papa trips!

Papa falls!

"We will find the real

Easter Bunny," says Mama.

The bears go looking for
the Easter Bunny.

They find the bunny's home.

They knock on his door.

The Easter Bunny comes out.

"What is it?" asks the bunny.

"We need you!" says Sister.

"We need Easter eggs!"

"I am resting," says the bunny.

"But we need you!" says Brother.

"We need the Easter Bunny!"

"Bunny!" says Honey.

"Yes!" sighs the bunny.

"I *am* the Easter Bunny!"

He pulls a rope.

A whistle blows.

Helper bunnies hop out.

They grab baskets of Easter eggs.

The helper bunnies hop off
with their Easter baskets.

Easter is really here!

The bears get Easter goodies.

"At last!" they all say.

"Yum! Yum! Yum!" says Honey.